W9-BMB-390

W9-BMB-390

The SECRETS of NINJA SCHOOL

Deb Pilutti

★ LEARN YOUR OWN ★ SECRET SKILL at MASTER WILLOW'S SCHOOL FOR NINJAS

MASTER WILLOW

THIS WEEKEND!

Christy Ottaviano Books

Henry Holt and Company • New York

Henry Holt and Company, *Publishers since 1866*
Henry Holt® is a registered trademark of Macmillan Publishing Group, LLC
175 Fifth Avenue, New York, NY 10010 • mackids.com

Copyright © 2018 by Deb Pilutti
All rights reserved.

Library of Congress Cataloging-in-Publication Data is available.
ISBN 978-1-62779-649-1

Our books may be purchased in bulk for promotional, educational, or business use.
Please contact your local bookseller or the Macmillan Corporate and Premium Sales Department at
(800) 221-7945 ext. 5442 or by e-mail at MacmillanSpecialMarkets@macmillan.com.

First edition, 2018 / Designed by Danielle Mazzella di Bosco
The illustrations for this book were created with gouache and pen and ink.
Printed in China by Toppan Leefung Printing Ltd., Dongguan City, Guangdong Province

1 3 5 7 9 10 8 6 4 2

For Kyle,
my ninja girl

Tucked outside the busiest
section of the village,

over a meandering brook,
across a wide yellow field of waving grass,

and up a steep,
craggy hill
sat a school.

Almost there!

THIS
WAY

NINJA
SCHOOL

It was dark most of the year, but
for one weekend each summer, boys
and girls came from all over the valley
to learn the ways of the *ninja*.

MASTER WILLOW

Master Willow called them "saplings."

They came to learn how to . . .
sneak, slither, and creep *invisibly*,
jump, kick, and throw *skillfully*,
sit, listen, and wait *patiently*,
and how to be *brave*.

But most of all, they came to Master
Willow's Schoo for Ninjas to discover
their very own secret skill.

The saplings learned quickly.
Except for Ruby.
When she sneaked, slithered, and crept,
Ruby was NOT invisible.

When she jumped,

kicked,

and threw,

Ruby was NOT skillful.

When she sat, listened, and waited,
Ruby was NOT patient.

And Ruby was most certainly
NOT brave.

If Ruby had a secret skill,
she did not know how to find it.

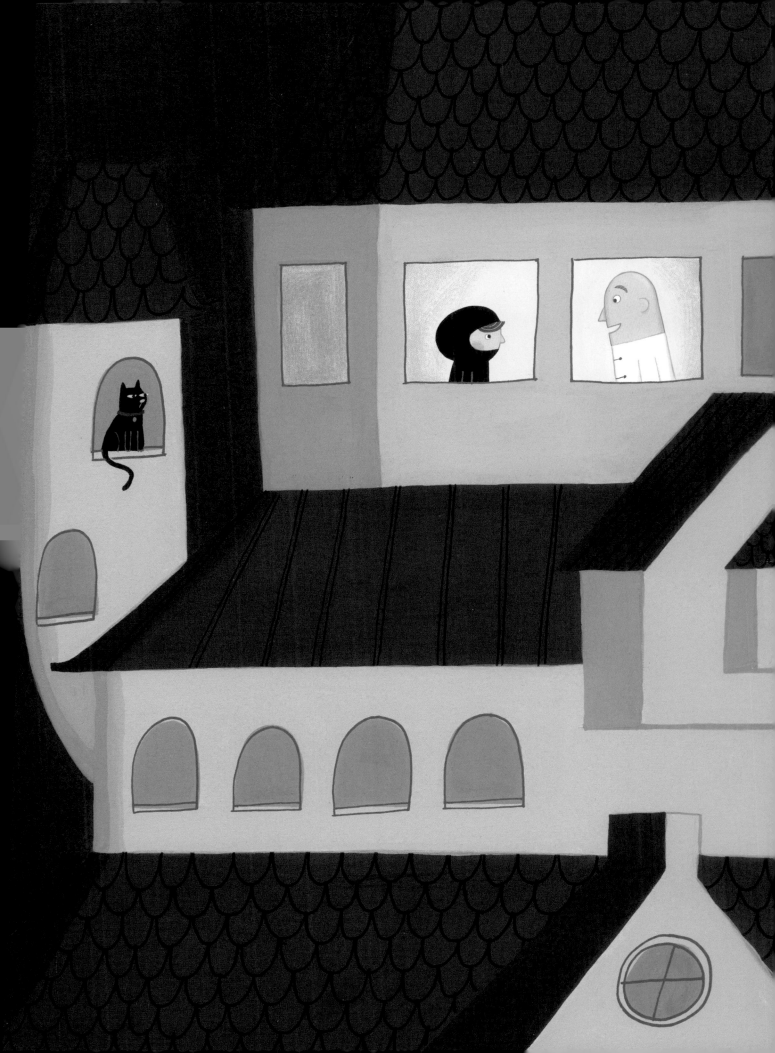

"Oh, Master Willow," said Ruby, "I will never be a ninja."

"Don't worry, sapling. You will improve."

"But I'm afraid," whispered Ruby.

"We are all afraid of something," said Master Willow.

"What if I don't have a secret skill?"

"Every sapling has one," said Master Willow. "It's a mystery to you now, but practicing the ways of the ninja will help you discover it."

Ruby practiced.
Even though she was getting
better, she felt no closer to finding
her secret skill.

Bedtime was the hardest. At the far side of night, when even the shadows sleep, Ruby lay wide awake. A teardrop rolled down one cheek and landed on the pillow—*plop!*— which woke the other saplings.

"What's wrong?" they asked.

"I'm homesick!" cried Ruby.

"Ninjas don't get homesick," said a sapling.

"Ninjas are brave," said another.

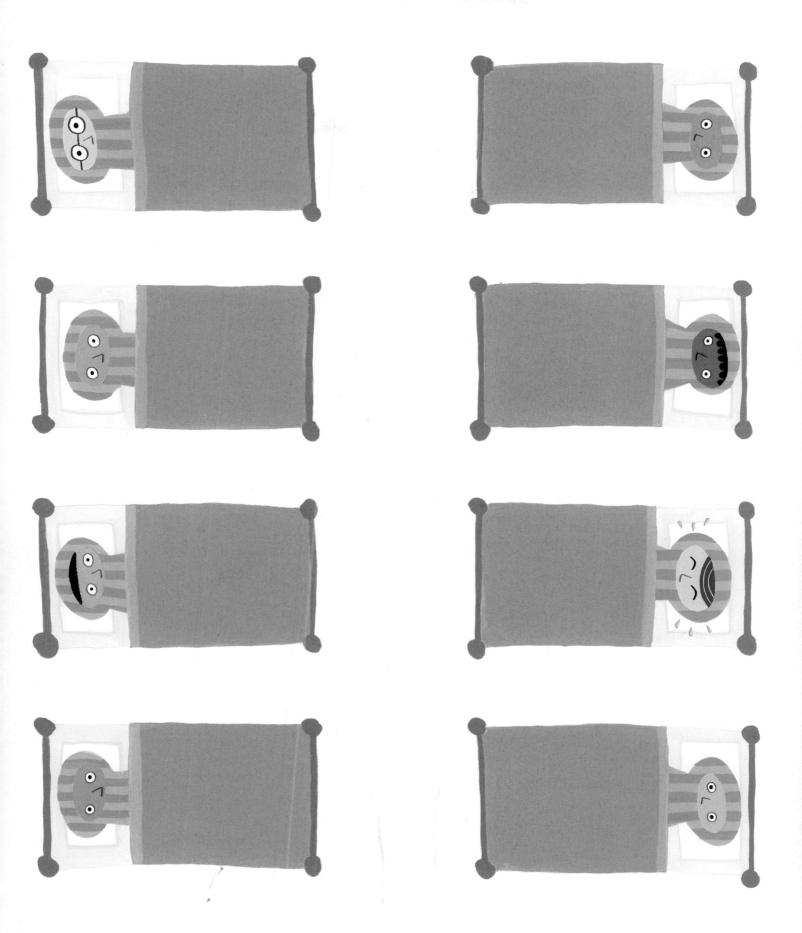

"But I miss my family!" said Ruby.

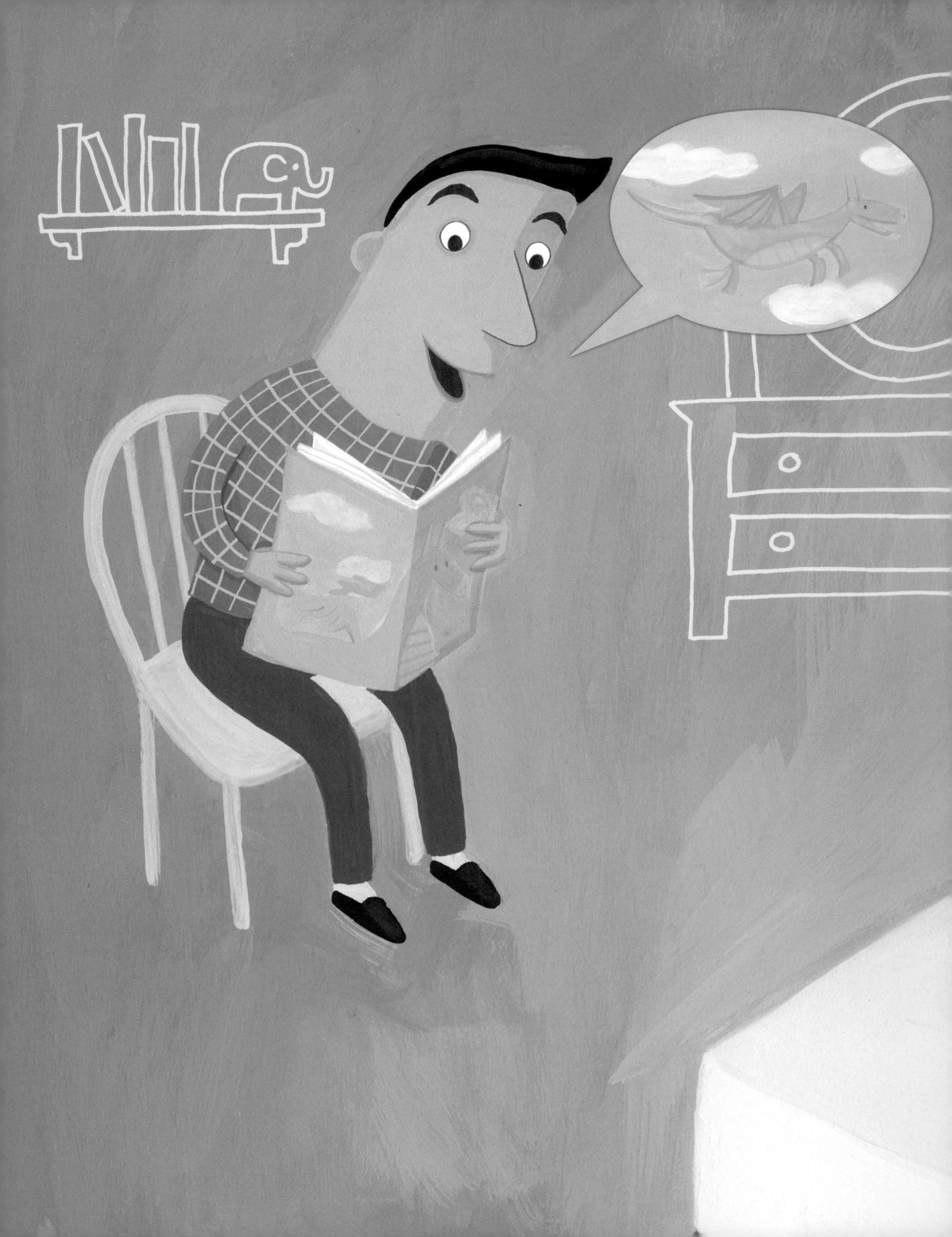

And Ruby told the saplings about how
when she was wide awake, like tonight,
Father would read her books filled with
tales of adventure.

Or when she was afraid of the dark,
like tonight, Mother would turn on a small
lamp and kiss Ruby on the very
tippiest part of her nose.

Or when she was feeling worried, like tonight,
Gran would bring out a big box heaped with material,
thread, and colored buttons, and they would
spend hours making the most
magnificent creations.

It was so quiet that Ruby thought the saplings had fallen back to sleep. But then she heard

a *sniff*

and a *gasp*

and a *WAIL*.

Before she knew it, all the other saplings were crying.

"Oh!" said Ruby. "You're homesick too."

"Nonsense!" cried one.

"Not me!" bawled another.

Ruby knew just what to do!

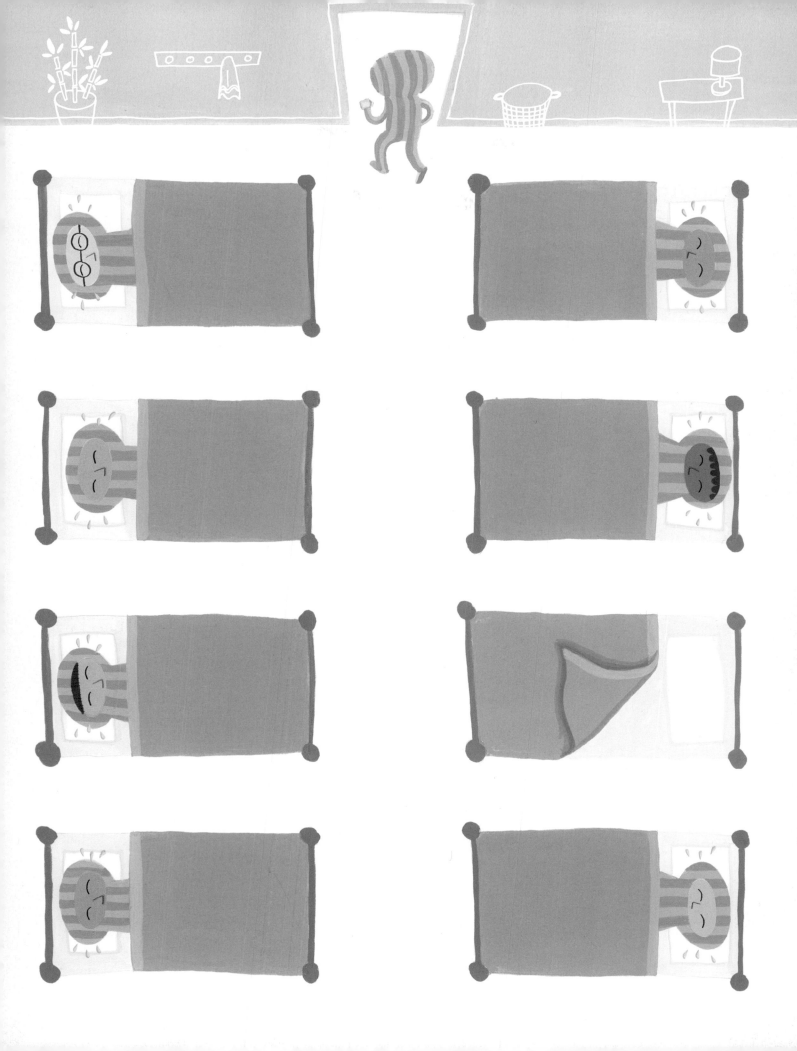

"Where are you going?" asked a sapling.

There was no answer.

"Let's follow," said another.

But Ruby was nowhere to be found. When she
sneaked down the hallway, Ruby was invisible.
When she jumped over obstacles, Ruby was skillful.

NINJA CRAFT AREA

When she snipped and stitched
and stuffed, Ruby was patient.

And when she crept back to her room through the silent, shadowy hallways, Ruby was very, very brave.

Ruby switched on a lamp, and the room
filled with a warm glow.
 She gave each of the saplings a stuffed
dragon and told them stories of bravery
and daring.

"Ruby, your skills are no longer a secret," exclaimed
Master Willow. "You are a wonderful storyteller, a fine
dragon maker, and a very good friend."

WELCOME SARDINES! NINJAS!

Ruby kept practicing, because being
brave isn't always easy.
Even for a ninja.

Make Your Own Dragon Softie

MATERIALS

3 different colors of felt:
    2 sheets for A and D
    1 sheet for B and C
    1 sheet for E
2 black buttons
straight pins
embroidery needle
embroidery floss
stuffing material

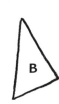

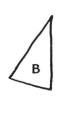

INSTRUCTIONS

1. Make a copy of the pattern pieces.
2. Using the patterns, cut pieces A, B, C, D, and E from felt.
3. Sew or glue buttons and pieces C, D, and E onto the front of body part A.
4. Pin the two body pieces together.

5. Pin the horns between the body pieces.
6. Using a straight stitch, sew around the body pieces, sewing through the horns. Leave an opening around the nose to fill with stuffing.
7. Add stuffing material.
8. Finish stitching around the nose.
9. Remove pins.

Pattern Pieces

A

(Cut 2 A pieces.)

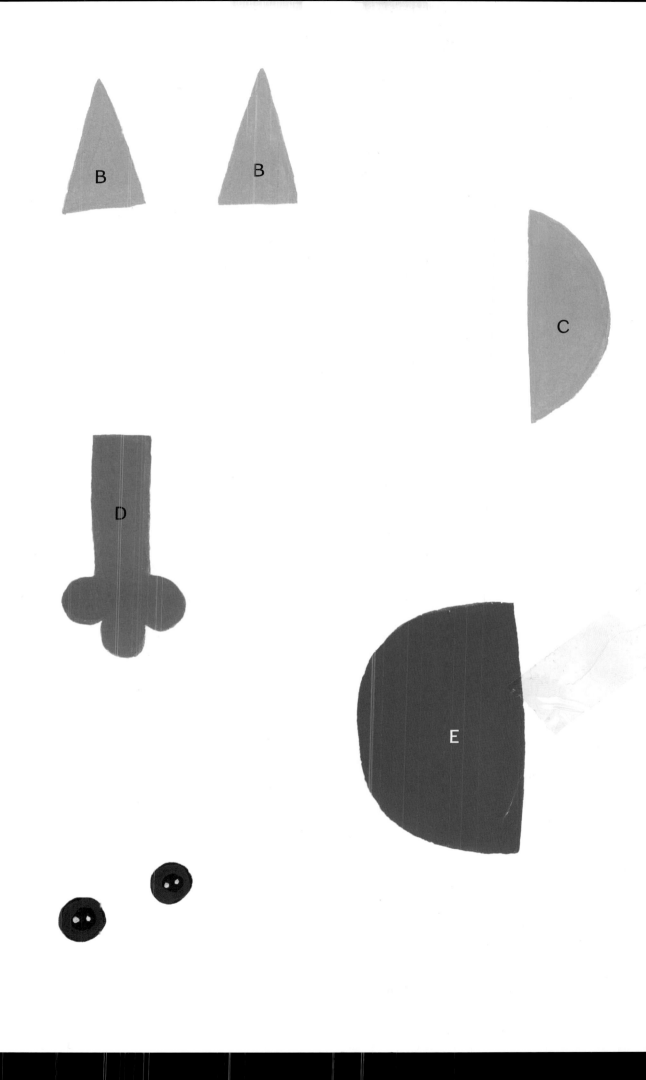

Make a No-Sew Dragon

MATERIALS

3 different colors of
construction paper:
   2 sheets for A and D
   1 sheet for B and C
   1 sheet for E
2 black buttons
hole punch
glue
yarn
stuffing material

INSTRUCTIONS

1. Make a copy of the
   pattern pieces.
2. Using the patterns,
   cut pieces A, B, C, D, and E from construction paper.
3. Glue the buttons and pieces B, C, D, and E to the dragon body (A).
4. Align the dragon body pieces and punch holes evenly around
   the edges.
5. Lace yarn through the holes. Leave an opening around the nose
   to fill with stuffing.
6. Add stuffing material.
7. Finish lacing around the nose and tie ends of yarn together.

TIP: Wrapping one end of the yarn with tape strengthens the end
and makes it easier to lace.